ALFRED's SACRED PERFORMER COLLECTIONS

MW00826914

Wondrous Praise
Book 4: Favorites from the Late 2000s

10 Arrangements of Praise and Worship

Arranged by James Koerts

I arranged these songs of praise from the late 2000s to move your listeners to meaningful moments of worship. As you prepare and perform these selections, please be mindful of the messages they convey, allowing that to guide your interpretation and musical expression. I hope that these arrangements enhance both your personal and group worship times.

James Koerts

Produced by
Alfred Music
P.O. Box 10003
Van Nuys, CA 91410-0003
alfred.com

Printed in USA.

No part of this book shall be reproduced, arranged, adapted, recorded, publicly performed, stored in a retrieval system, or transmitted by any means without written permission from the publisher. In order to comply with copyright laws, please apply for such written permission and/or license by contacting the publisher at alfred.com/permissions.

ISBN-10: 0-7390-8904-8
ISBN-13: 978-0-7390-8904-0

Cover Photo
Happy cheering celebrating success woman at beautiful sunset © Shutterstock.com / Maridav

(Approx. Performance Time – 3:00)

10,000 Reasons
(Bless the Lord)

Words and Music by
Matt Redman and Jonas Myrin
Arr. James Koerts

© 2011 SHOUT! PUBLISHING (APRA) (Administered in the U.S. and Canada at EMICMGPublishing.com), THANKYOU MUSIC (PRS)
(Administered worldwide at EMICMGPublishing.com excluding Europe which is Administered. by kingswaysongs.com), WORSHIPTOGETHER.
COM SONGS, SIXSTEPS MUSIC and SAID AND DONE MUSIC (Administered at EMICMGPublishing.com)
All Rights Reserved   Used by Permission

(Approx. Performance Time – 2:15)

Amazing Grace
(My Chains Are Gone)

Words and Music by
Chris Tomlin and Louie Giglio
Arr. James Koerts

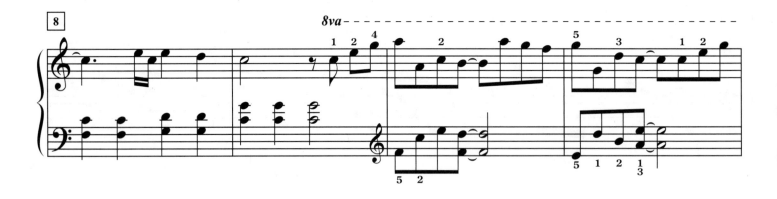

© 2006 WORSHIPTOGETHER.COM SONGS, SIXSTEPS MUSIC and VAMOS PUBLISHING
All Rights Administered at EMICMGPublishing.com
All Rights Reserved   Used by Permission

(Approx. Performance Time – 3:15)

How Can I Keep from Singing

Words and Music by
Chris Tomlin, Ed Cash and Matt Redman
Arr. James Koerts

With joy (♩. = 69–72)

© 2006 THANKYOU MUSIC (PRS) (Administered Worldwide at EMICMGPublishing.com excluding Europe, which is Administered by Kingswaysongs.com), WORSHIPTOGETHER.COM SONGS, SIXSTEPS MUSIC (Administered at EMICMGPublishing.com) and ALLETROP MUSIC (Administered by MUSIC SERVICES, INC.)
All Rights Reserved   Used by Permission

(Approx. Performance Time – 2:45)

I Will Follow

Words and Music by
Chris Tomlin, Jason Ingram, and Reuben Morgan
Arr. James Koerts

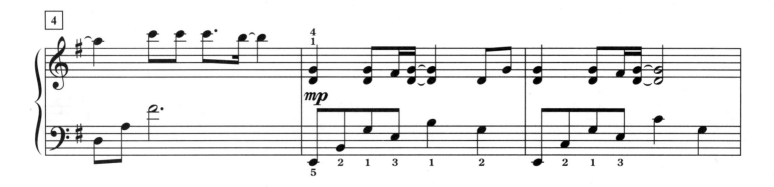

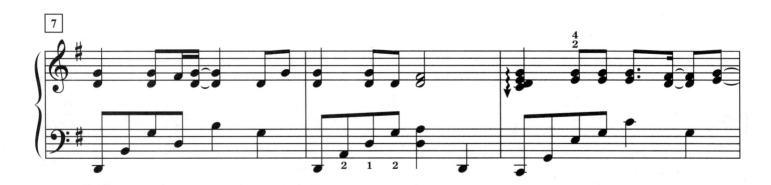

© 2010 SHOUT! PUBLISHING (APRA) (Administered in the US and Canada at EMICMGPublishing.com) WORSHIPTOGETHER.COM
SONG (ASCAP), SIXSTEP MUSIC (ASCAP), VAMOS PUBLISHING (ASCAP)
(Administered at EMICMGPublishing.com) and SONY/ATV TIMBER PUB. (SESAC)
All Rights Reserved   Used By Permission

(Approx. Performance Time – 4:45)

I Will Rise

Words and Music by Chris Tomlin,
Jesse Reeves, Louie Giglio and Matt Maher
Arr. James Koerts

Gently, with expression ($\quarternote = 76$)

© 2008 THANKYOU MUSIC (PRS) (Administered worldwide at EMICMGPublishing.com excluding Europe which is Administered by
KINGSWAYSONGS), WORSHIPTOGETHER.COM SONGS, SIXSTEPS MUSIC. SPIRITANDSONG.COM PUBLISHING
and VAMOS PUBLISHING
All Rights for WORSHIPTOGETHER.COM SONGS, SIXSTEPS MUSIC. SPIRITANDSONG.COM PUBLISHING
and VAMOS PUBLISHING Administered at EMICMGPublishing.com
All Rights Reserved   Used by Permission

(Approx. Performance Time – 4:15)

Jesus Messiah

Words and Music by Daniel Carson,
Chris Tomlin, Ed Cash and Jesse Reeves
Arr. James Koerts

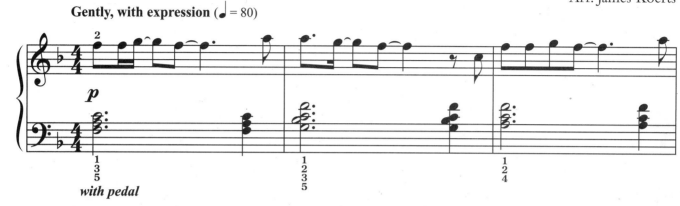

© 2008 WORSHIPTOGETHER.COM SONGS, SIXSTEPS MUSIC, VAMOS PUBLISHING and ALLETROP MUSIC
All Rights for WORSHIPTOGETHER.COM SONGS, SIXSTEPS MUSIC and VAMOS PUBLISHING Administered at EMICMGPublishing.com
All Rights for ALLETROP MUSIC Administered by MUSIC SERVICES, INC.
All Rights Reserved   Used by Permission

(Approx. Performance Time – 3:00)

Our God

Words and Music by Jesse Reeves,
Chris Tomlin, Matt Redman and Jonas Myrin
Arr. James Koerts

© 2010 SHOUT! PUBLISHING (APRA), WORSHIPTOGETHER.COM SONGS (ASCAP) SIXSTEPS MUSIC (ASCAP), VAMOS
PUBLISHING (ASCAP) and SAID AND DONE MUSIC (ASCAP) (Administered at EMICMGPublishing.com) THANKYOU MUSIC (PRS)
(Administered worldwide at EMICMGPublishing.com excluding Europe which is Administered. by kingswaysongs.com)
All Rights Reserved   Used by Permission

(Approx. Performance Time – 3:00)

Sing, Sing, Sing

Words and Music by Chris Tomlin, Daniel Carson,
Jesse Reeves, Matt Gilder and Travis Nunn
Arr. James Koerts

© 2008 WORSHIPTOGETHER.COM SONGS, SIXSTEPS MUSIC, VAMOS PUBLISHING and RYAN HOUSE PUBLISHING
All Rights for WORSHIPTOGETHER.COM SONGS, SIXSTEPS MUSIC and VAMOS PUBLISHING Administered at EMICMGPublishing.com
All Rights for RYAN HOUSE PUBLISHING Administered by Music Services, Inc.
All Rights Reserved Used by Permission

(Approx. Performance Time – 2:30)

Your Name

Words and Music by
Glenn Packiam and Paul Baloche
Arr. James Koerts

© 2006 INTEGRITY'S HOSANNA! MUSIC (ASCAP), VERTICAL WORSHIP SONGS (ASCAP) (Administered at EMICMGPublishing.com)
All Rights Reserved   Used By Permission

(Approx. Performance Time – 3:30)

Stronger

Words and Music by
Ben Fielding and Reuben Morgan
Arr. James Koerts

© 2007 HILLSONG MUSIC PUBLISHING (APRA) (Administered in the US and Canada at EMICMGPublishing.com)
All Rights Reserved   Used By Permission